LAURENCE ANHOLT has been described as "one of the most versatile writers for children today" and was included in *The Independent On Sunday* "Top 10 Children's Authors in Britain." From his home in Lyme Regis, he has produced more than 90 children's titles, which are published in dozens of languages around the world, many of them in collaboration with his wife, Catherine. His books range from the "Anholt Artists" series to the irrepressible *Chimp and Zee*. Laurence has won numerous awards, including the Nestlé Smarties Gold Award on two occasions.

Laurence and Catherine Anholt are the owners of *Chimp and Zee, Bookshop by the Sea* in Lyme Regis. Stocked entirely with their own signed books, prints, and cards, and crammed with automated displays and book-related exhibits, it is one of the most magical children's bookshops you could ever hope to visit.

First edition for the United States,
Canada, and the Philippines published 1994
by Barron's Educational Series, Inc.

First published in Great Britain in 1994
by Frances Lincoln Limited, 4 Torriano Mews,
Torriano Avenue, London NW5 2RZ

All inquiries should be addressed to:
Barron's Educational Series, Inc.
250 Wireless Boulevard
Hauppauge, New York 11788

The Library of Congress has catalogued the
hardcover editions as follows:
Library of Congress Catalog Card No. 94-5227

ISBN-13: 978-0-7641-3854-6
ISBN-10: 0-7641-3854-5

Library of Congress Cataloging-in-Publication Data
Anholt, Laurence.
Camille and the sunflowers / Laurence Anholt.—1st ed.
p. cm.
Summary: Despite the derision of their
neighbors, a young French boy and his family
befriend the lonely painter who comes to their
town and begin to admire his unusual paintings.

1. Gogh, Vincent van, 1853-1890—Juvenile fiction. [1. Gogh,
Vincent van, 1853-1890—Fiction. 2. Artists—Fiction.
3. Friendship—Fiction 4. France—Fiction.] I. Title.
PZ7.A5863 Cam 1994
[Fic]—dc20

94-5227
CIP
AC

Date of manufacture: March 2011
Manufactured by: Kwong Fat Offset Printing, Dongguan, Guangdong, China
19 18 17 16 15 14 13 12 11 10 9 8 7 6 5 4

For Cathy
With Love

The Postman Roulin (Collection:
State Museum Kröller-Müller, Otterlo,
The Netherlands); **La Berceuse** (Museum of Fine
Arts, Boston); **Armand Roulin** (Museum Folkwang, Essen);
Roulin's Baby (Chester Dale Collection, National Gallery
of Art, Washington); **Portrait of Camille Roulin**
(Museu de Arte de São Paolo Assis Chateaubriand;
photograph by Luiz Hossaka); **Vase with 14 Sunflowers**
and **Self-portrait with Grey Felt Hat**
(Collection Vincent van Gogh Foundation/
Van Gogh Museum, Amsterdam).

van Gogh
and the Sunflowers

A story about Vincent van Gogh

by LAURENCE ANHOLT

WHERE Camille lived, the sunflowers grew so high they looked like real suns —

a whole field of burning yellow suns.

Every day after school Camille ran through the sunflowers to meet his father, who was a postman. Together they would lift down the heavy sacks of mail.

627

One day a strange man arrived in Camille's town. He had a straw hat, a yellow beard, and quick brown eyes.

“I am Vincent, the painter,” he said, smiling at Camille.

Vincent came to live in the yellow house at the end of Camille’s street.

He had no money and no friends.

"Let's try to help him," said Camille's father.

So they loaded the cart with pots and pans and furniture for the yellow house.

Camille picked a huge bunch of sunflowers for the painter and put them in a big brown pot.

Vincent was very pleased to have two good friends.

Vincent asked Camille's father if he would like to have his picture painted dressed in his best blue uniform.

"You must sit very still," said Vincent.

Camille loved the bright colors Vincent used and the strong smell of paint.

As Camille watched, his father's face appeared like magic on the canvas.

The picture was strange but very beautiful.

Vincent said he would like to paint the whole family —

Camille's mother,

his big brother,

his baby sister,...

and at last, Camille himself.

Camille was very excited — he had never even had his picture taken with a camera.

Camille took his painting to school. He wanted everyone to see it.

But the other children didn't like the picture. They all began to laugh.

This made Camille feel very sad.

After school some of the older children started teasing Vincent.

They ran along behind him as he went out to paint.

Even the grown-ups joined in. "It's time he got a real job," they said, "instead of playing with paints all day."

Camille sat for hours watching Vincent work. It was very hot but Vincent worked fast. He painted the sunflower fields and even the sun itself.

"He is the Sunflower Man," said Camille to himself.

But no matter how hard Vincent worked, he could never sell any of his paintings.

"If I had a lot of money," said Camille, "I would like to buy them all."

"Thank you, my friend," laughed Vincent.

One afternoon, as Camille and Vincent were coming back from the fields, some of the children from Camille's school were waiting.

They shouted at Vincent and threw stones at him.

Camille wanted them to stop — but what could he do? He was only a small boy. At last he ran home in tears.

"Listen, Camille," said his father, "people often laugh at things that are different, but I've got a feeling that one day they will learn to love Vincent's paintings."

That night, Camille
had a strange dream.
He saw Vincent standing
in the moonlight
high above the town.

Vincent had stuck candles on his hat so that he could see.

The Sunflower Man was painting the stars!

Early the next morning, Camille was awakened by a loud knocking at the door.

Some men from the town had come to see his father.

"Listen, Postman," they said, "we want you to give this letter to your friend. It says he must pack up his paints and leave our town."

Camille slipped out through the back door. He ran down the street to the yellow house.

It seemed very quiet inside.

Then Camille saw the sunflowers he had picked for Vincent — they had all dried up and died. Camille felt sadder than ever.

Vincent was upstairs packing his bags. He looked very tired but he smiled at Camille.

"Don't be sad," he said. "It's time for me to paint somewhere else now. Perhaps they will like my paintings there."

"But first I have something to show you...."

Vincent lifted down a big picture.
There were Camille's sunflowers,
bigger and brighter than ever!

Camille looked at the painting.
Then he smiled too.

"Goodbye, Sunflower Man,"
he whispered, and ran out of the
yellow house and into the sunshine.

Camille's father was right. People did learn to love Vincent's paintings. Today you would have to have a lot of money if you wanted to buy one. But now people all over the world go to museums and galleries just to see Vincent's paintings of *The Yellow House*, of Camille and his family, and especially the picture of *The Sunflowers* — so bright and yellow, they look like real suns.

Vincent van Gogh was born in Holland on March 30, 1853. As a young man, Vincent studied to become a clergyman like his father. He was 27 before he began to paint seriously. At the age of 35, Vincent went to the south of France looking for sunshine and brighter colors. Here he became friends with Camille's family. During this time he painted more than 150 pictures, although only one was sold in his lifetime.

Vincent became lonely and ill and at last, in a fit of madness, tried to cut off his own ear. He was taken to the hospital, but even there he kept on painting. In May 1890, he traveled north to Auvers-sur-Oise to seek help from another doctor. But only two months later he shot himself with a pistol. He died on July 29, and was buried in the local churchyard, far away from the sunshine and color he had come to love so dearly.